In a village on the great plain in India, there once lived a farmer with three lazy sons.

The farmer had a field where he planted wheat but his sons
never helped him.

The farmer's wife was upset with her lazy sons. They sat in the house all day dreaming about gold but never doing any work.

She scolded them, but they would not listen. All they ever said in reply was, "We don't want to be farmers. We just want to make a lot of gold."

Finally the farmer's wife thought of a plan. "My sons," she said to them, "there is a secret that I have not told you. Long ago, my father buried a treasure of gold in this field. If you find it, you may have it all."

The sons looked up with interest.
"How deep is the treasure buried?" asked the first son.
"Where in the field is it buried?" asked the second son.

"What should we do to find it?" asked the third son.
"I am not sure," she said. "Maybe if you plow the field, you will find it."

The next morning, the farmer's sons were in the field before
the morning mists had lifted. They hitched oxen to their
plows and began to dig up the hard earth.

"Rest," said the farmer's wife to her husband. "Let your sons plow the field. They are young and you are old. It is time they worked for their living." The farmer smiled at her and together they watched their sons working hard in the field.

That evening, the sons returned looking sad.
"What is the matter my sons?" asked the farmer's wife.

"We did not find the treasure," said the first son.
"It must be buried deeper than the plow can reach," said the second son.
"What can we do to find it?" asked the third son.

"Maybe if you plant these seeds, the roots will dig down deep enough to curl around the gold and pull it up. They are very special seeds," said the farmer's wife.

The farmer looked at the seeds in his wife's hand and smiled. "These seeds are special indeed," he said.

Early the next morning, the farmer showed his sons how to sow seeds. All day long, his sons sowed the special seeds. That evening they were too tired to talk.

The next morning, they looked out at the field hoping to see their gold. They turned to their mother with faces as long as wheat sheaves. "What is the matter my sons?" asked the farmer's wife. "You do not look happy this morning."

"The seeds have not sprouted yet," said the first son.
"Our gold has not been pulled up yet," said the second son.
"What can we do to help the roots reach the gold and pull it up?" asked the third son.

"Water the field," said the farmer's wife.

All day the sons dug a ditch to bring fresh river water to the field.

That evening they returned with smiles on their faces.
"You are smiling, my sons," said the farmer's wife.

"The smell of wet earth is wonderful," said the first son.
"The sparkle of the water is beautiful," said the second son.
"Should we do the same tomorrow?" asked the third son.

"Yes," said the farmer's wife. "Your father will show you how to tend the seeds until they pull the treasure up by their roots."

The next day, the farmer's sons sang as they worked. The sun beat down on their backs, but they enjoyed feeling the soft, rich earth between their fingers.

They were in the field every day, tending the plants that would one day grow strong roots and pull the hidden treasure out of the soil. They worked from early dawn to late dusk. Some nights, they lay in bed too tired to think.

The farmer watched them growing strong in their bodies
and in their love for the land.

One morning, as the first ray of sunlight broke through the clouds, the first son looked out upon the fields and saw something sparkling.

"Gold, gold!" he shouted. "My brothers, we have our gold at last!"

The other two rushed to the window.

As far as the eye could see, stalks of wheat were waving in the morning sun. The field was a sea of grain.

At last, the three sons understood what the treasure was that had been hidden in the ground. "Mother, the treasure that was buried has surfaced at last," said the first son.

"Mother, the seeds have reached deeper than we thought they could," said the second son. "They have pulled to the surface something that slept within us."

"Father, can you show us how to harvest the grain?" asked
the third son.

The farmer turned to his wife with a smile of thanks on his face. Then he went out with his three hardworking sons to reap the golden harvest.